In memory of my mother and her pies — C.A.

There is more than chocolate in life, there are cookies! — S.J.

Text copyright © 2020 by Caroline Adderson
Illustrations copyright © 2020 by Stéphane Jorisch

Tundra Books, an imprint of Penguin Random House Canada Young Readers, a Penguin Random House Company

Library and Archives Canada Cataloguing in Publication

Title: It happened on Sweet Street / Caroline Adderson ; illustrated by Stéphane Jorisch.
Names: Adderson, Caroline, 1963- author. | Jorisch, Stéphane, illustrator.
Identifiers: Canadiana (print) 20190098074 | Canadiana (ebook) 20190098082 | ISBN 9781101918852
(hardcover) | ISBN 9781101918869 (EPUB)
Classification: LCC PS8551.D3267 I84 2020 | DDC jC813/.54—dc23

Published simultaneously in the United States of America by Tundra Books of Northern New York, an imprint of Penguin Random House Canada Young Readers, a Penguin Random House Company

Library of Congress Control Number: 2019939486

Edited by Tara Walker with assistance from Margot Blankier
Designed by John Martz
The artwork in this book was rendered in pencil, ink and watercolor, and assembled digitally.
The text was set in LTC Powell.

Printed and bound in China

www.penguinrandomhouse.ca

2 3 4 5   24 23 22 21 20

tundra | Penguin Random House | TUNDRA BOOKS

It Happened on Sweet Street

written by CAROLINE ADDERSON • illustrated by STÉPHANE JORISCH

tundra

In the cul-de-sac on Sweet Street, there
were three shops, but only one sold treats.
It stood between the bric-a-brac boutique and
the shoemaker — the bakery owned by Monsieur
Oliphant, Exclusive Creator of Cakes.

Voilà the masterful Monsieur Oliphant!

In his kitchen, he jelly-rolled his cakes.

He layered them and cherried them and married people on them.

Every day cake customers lined up to buy Monsieur Oliphant's creations.

Eventually the old shoemaker on Sweet Street retired.
Monsieur Oliphant baked him a cake in the shape of
a boot with a dozen marzipan children living inside.

"*Adieu!*" he said.

And who moved into the shoemaker's shop? Mademoiselle Fée, a baker as well, but a Cookie Concocter *par excellence*!

Voilà the marvelous Biscuits à la Fée!

In her kitchen, Mademoiselle stamped her ingenious shapes.

She tooled them and jeweled them . . .

and dusted them
with sugar.

Monsieur Oliphant was not pleased.

He got busy baking even better cakes, trying to out-create Mademoiselle Fée.

For several months after that,
the cul-de-sac was
doubly crowded.

Customers lined the sidewalks on either side,
half of them eager for cake, the other cookies.

Then the dealer of bric-a-brac grew old, too old to sell her china and silver spoons. When she retired, Mademoiselle Fée created a replica for her, in gingerbread, of every figurine she'd ever sold.

"Bonne chance!" she said.

SMACK

And who moved into the bric-a-brac boutique?

Madame Clotilde, a baker too, but of pies.

Voilà the divine Pâtisserie Clotilde!

In her kitchen, Madame rolling-pinned her famous crust.
She frilled it and filled it with blackbirds and dancing ladies.

Monsieur Oliphant and Mademoiselle Fée
were not pleased.

In a frenzy, the two bakers baked, hoping
to out-concoct Madame Clotilde.

Now the cul-de-sac was absolutely packed
from morning to night every day of the week.

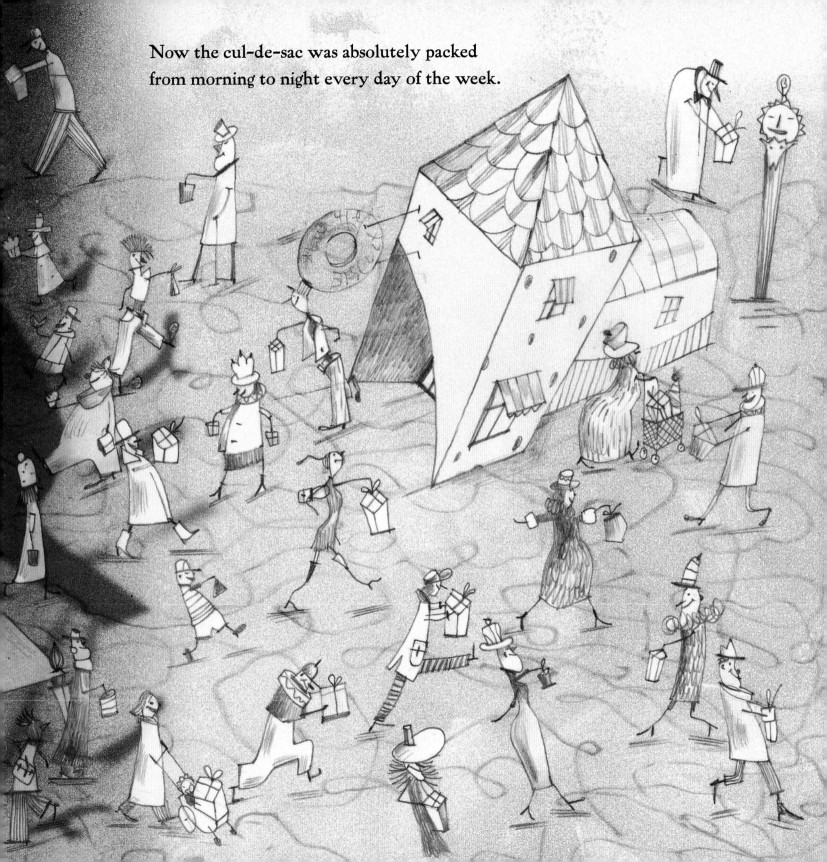

What happened on Sweet Street happened one sunny day when everyone was crowded together, arguing for their favorite dessert.

Monsieur Oliphant, hearing the commotion, stepped outside. Mademoiselle Fée did the same. They locked eyes in a glare.

And out of Pâtisserie Clotilde
stepped the baker of pies . . .

Was it on purpose, or by accident? No one knew . . .

Madame Clotilde's pie went flying.

Monsieur Oliphant was not pleased.

Neither was Mademoiselle Fée. Both bakers rushed inside their shops. They stepped out again, armed with desserts.

Within minutes, Sweet Street became a massacre of cream, a catastrophe of meringue, a devastation of crumbs.

Off to the side, clear of the battle,
a little girl found a half-crushed pie.

On top of it she nestled
a smooshed cake.

A cookie here. A cookie there. And . . . *voilà*!

The crowd stopped fighting and formed a silent circle around the girl and her astonishing creation. Even the three bakers fell back in awe.

Délicieuse!!!

Sweet Street has always
been a tasty place, but now
it's also a street of peace.
Everyone cheerfully lines up
for the dessert they prefer that
particular day. Cookies are
nice, but so is cake. Pie too.

They all taste sweet.